DATE DUE 9/18

For Hazel(nut), my own little star

Special thanks to Ranida and the McKneally family

The illustrations for this book were done in Turner Design Gouache on Arches 100% Rag Watercolor Paper 140 lb. Hot Press Bright White. This book was edited by Alvina Ling and designed by Jen Keenan with art direction by Saho Fujii. The production was supervised by Erika Schwartz, and the production editor was Annie McDonnell. The text was set in Loire, and the display type was hand-lettered by Jen Keenan.

A BIG Mooncake
for Little Star

GRACE LIN

Ⓛ Ⓑ

LITTLE, BROWN AND COMPANY

NEW YORK   BOSTON

LITTLE STAR'S mama laid the Big Mooncake onto the night sky to cool.

"Now, Little Star," Mama said, "your Mooncake took us a long time to bake, so let's see if you can make it last awhile. Can you remember not to touch this Big Mooncake until I tell you to?"

"Yes, Mama!" Little Star said, nodding.

And Little Star remembered
as she brushed her teeth,

washed her face,

snuggled into bed,

and fell asleep.

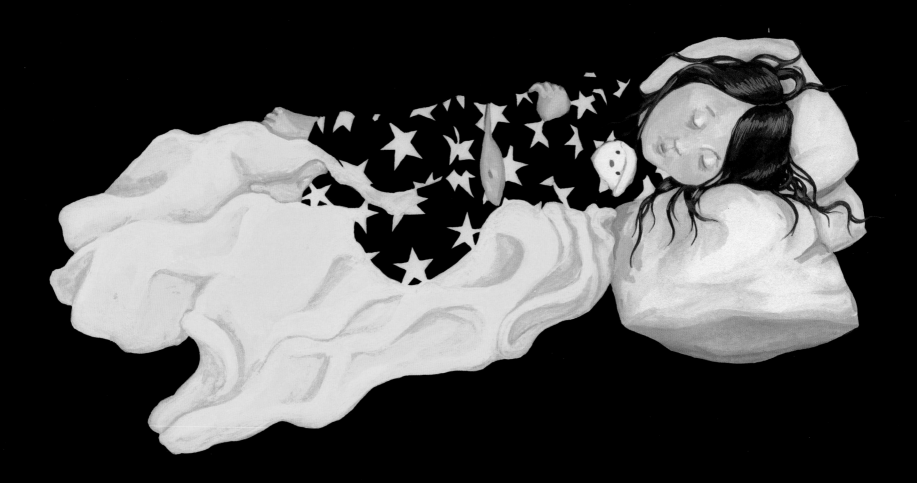

But in the middle of the night, Little Star woke up.

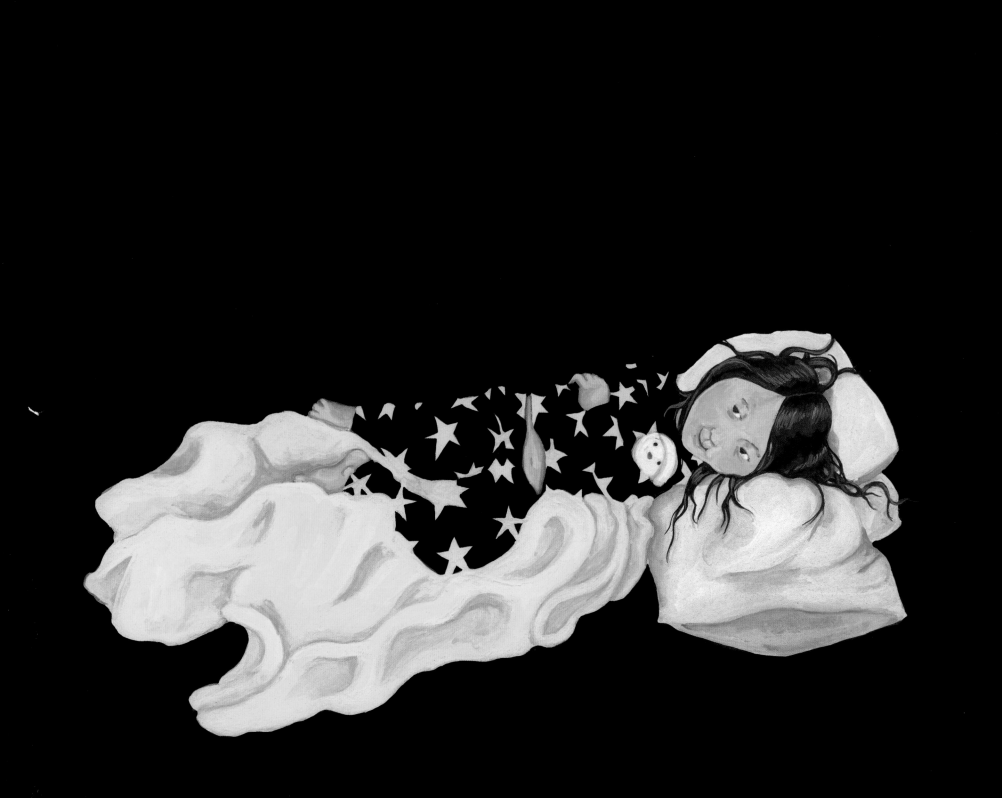

She forgot everything her mama had said
and only remembered the Big Mooncake.

Pat   *pat*   *pat.*

Little Star's soft feet tiptoed to the Big Mooncake.

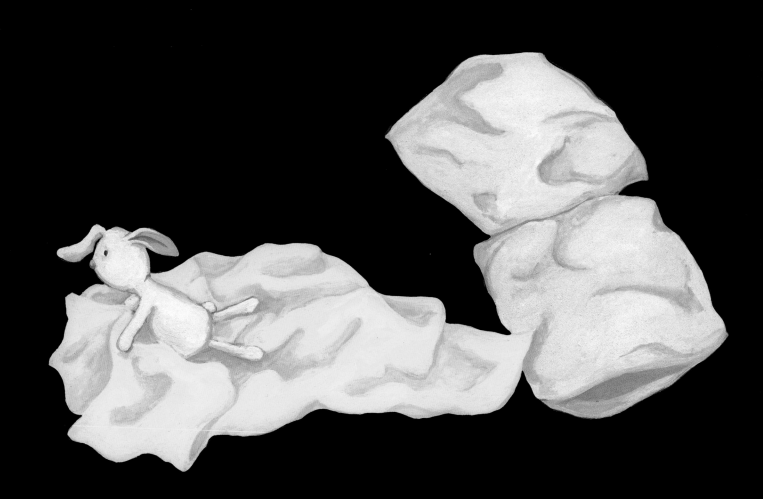

Would her mama notice if she took a tiny nibble?

Little Star didn't think so.

Mmmmm, yum!

But was someone coming?

Little Star flew back to bed.

The next night, Little Star remembered the Big Mooncake again.
That one bite had been so sweet and tasty! Was the cake still there?

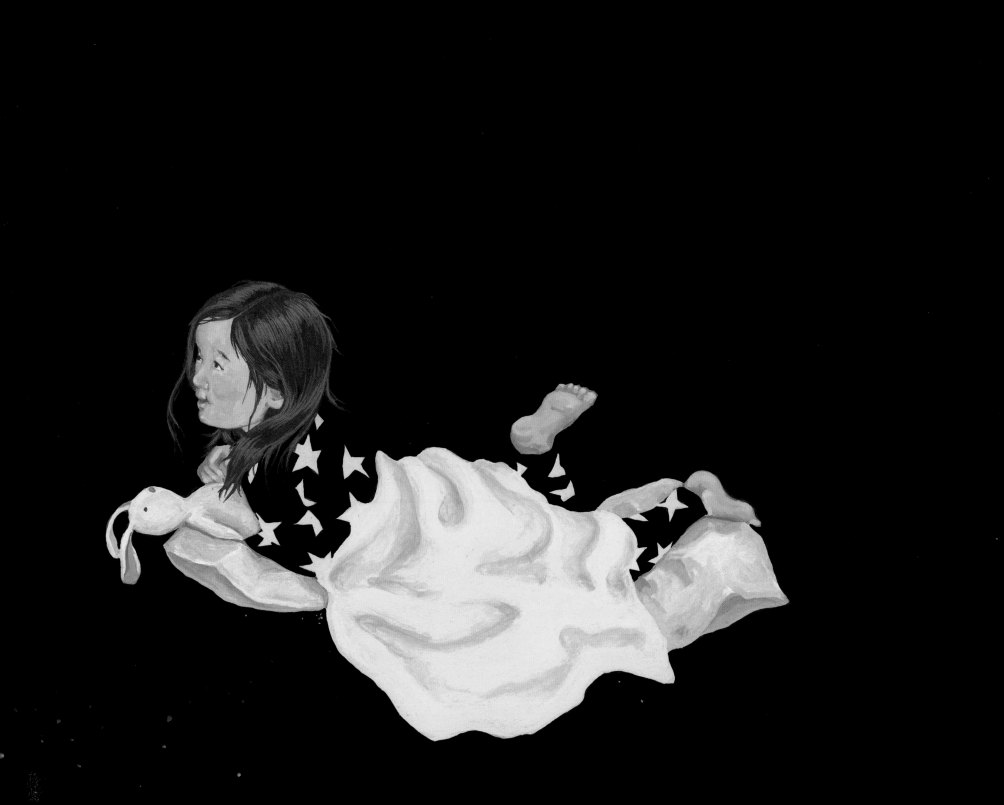

Yes, it was! There was that Big Mooncake, an almost perfect circle all alone and delicious in the sky. Would her mama notice if she took another tiny nibble? Little Star didn't think so.

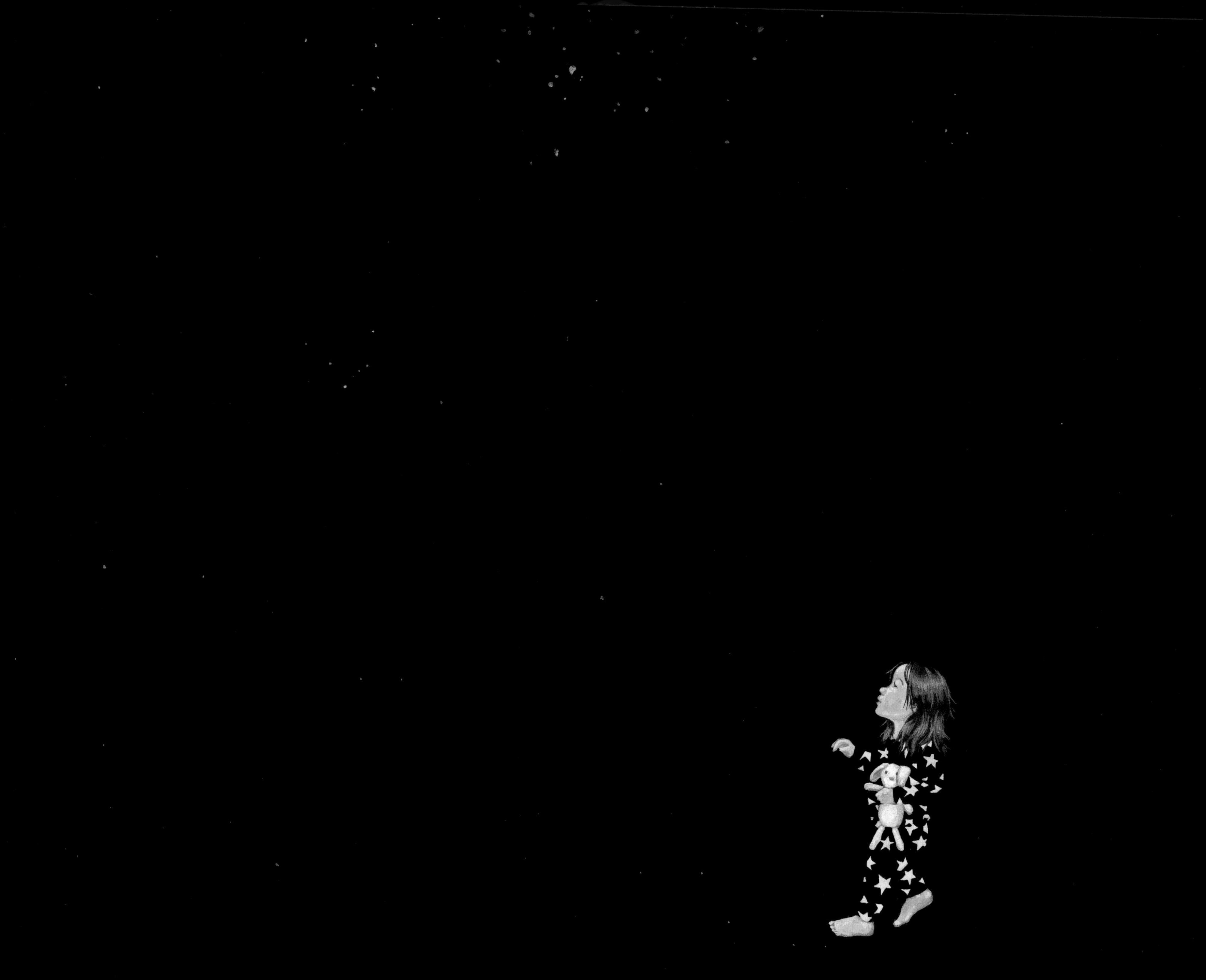

Yum! Little Star flew back to bed.

And the next night, what do you think Little Star remembered?
The Big Mooncake, of course! Would Mama notice if she took
another tiny nibble? Little Star didn't think so.

And the night after that, what did Little Star do?

Nibble, nibble . . . *yum!*

Night

after

night,

Little Star took tiny nibble
after tiny nibble
of the Big Mooncake.

Until one night, Little Star's mama went to look for the Big
Mooncake. Where was it? It was gone! Instead of a glowing,
round cake, there was just a trail of twinkling crumbs.

"Little Star!" her mama said, shaking her head even though her mouth was curving. "You ate the Big Mooncake again, didn't you?"

Little Star looked up, her grin reflecting her mama's smile.

"Yes, Mama," Little Star said, nodding.

"Now let's go make another one!"